A BALLOON AWAY

by ROSA PARK

FR

Sona is asleep.

A picture of a silver balloon is framed on her bedroom wall.

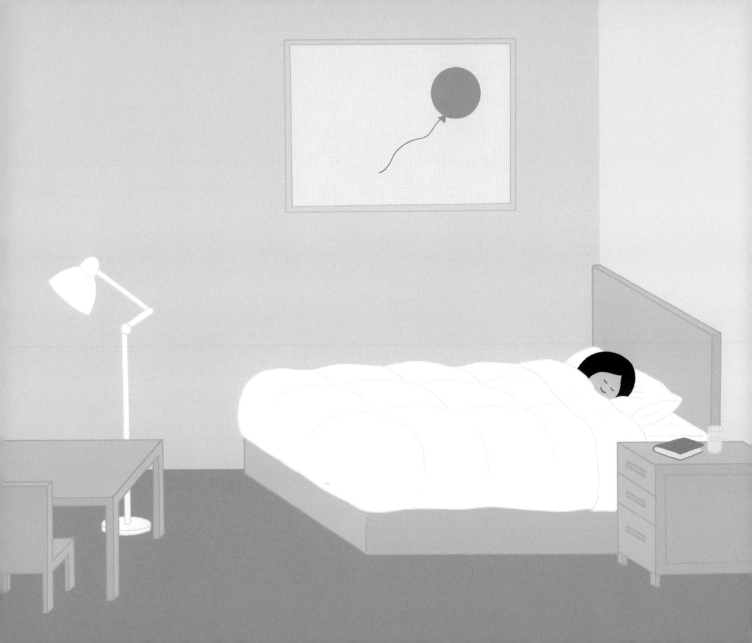

She lives in the city, in a tall building with many windows.

Through her window, she likes looking out at the world.

Ding Dong.

Sona wakes up to the sound of the doorbell.

It's her birthday today. She's excited to eat cake and open gifts.

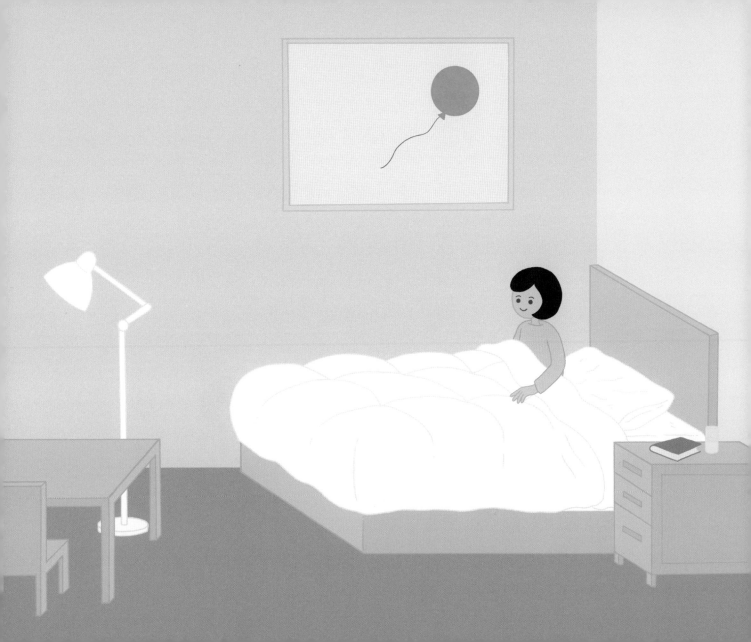

She jumps out of bed and tip toes to the front door.

A tiny grey bear is waiting for her.

Dear Sona

The tiny grey bear has a balloon and an envelope for Sona.

Inside the envelope, there is a letter.

Dear Sona,

Happy Birthday!
Let's go on an adventure!

Love, Grey

Sona takes the balloon from Grey. It's silver.

She feels floaty.

All of a sudden, she's flying through the air!

Grey is holding her hand.

In the distance, she spots something golden.

They land on sand.

A camel is walking across the dunes.

A camel can go up to seven months without drinking water.

Sona is impressed. She drinks five glasses of water a day.

She thinks she wouldn't make a very good camel.

With Grey and her silver balloon, Sona flies away to somewhere new.

In the distance, she spots something green.

They land on grass.

There is a lake, and mountains in the distance. There are trees everywhere.

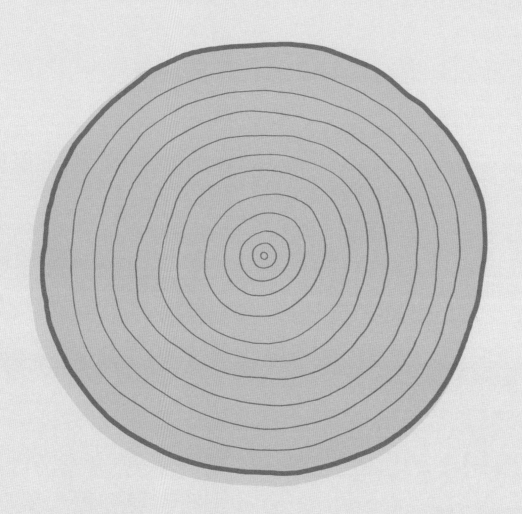

A tree's age can be determined by counting the number of rings in its trunk.

Sona knows how old she is by counting the number of candles on her cake.

With Grey and her silver balloon, Sona flies away to somewhere new.

In the distance, she spots something blue.

They land on the shore.

A big ocean and a sunny sky meet on the horizon.

A parasol looks like an umbrella. But it protects you from the sun instead of the rain.

Sona loves sunshine, but knows she has to be careful.

Getting sunburnt is no fun.

With Grey and her silver balloon, she flies away to somewhere new.

In the distance, she spots something white.

They land on ice.

An iceberg drifts in the cold water.

An iceberg is 90 per cent under water. Only the top part peeks out.

Sona thinks icebergs must be quite shy.

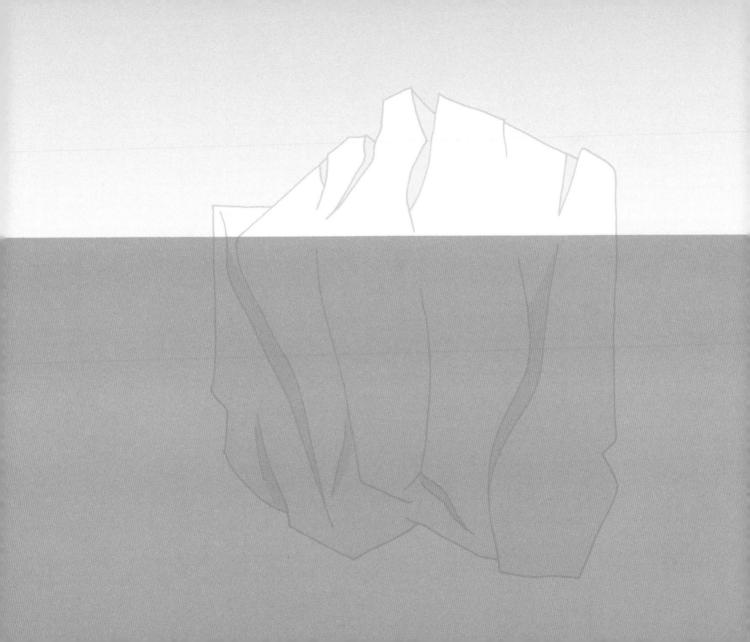

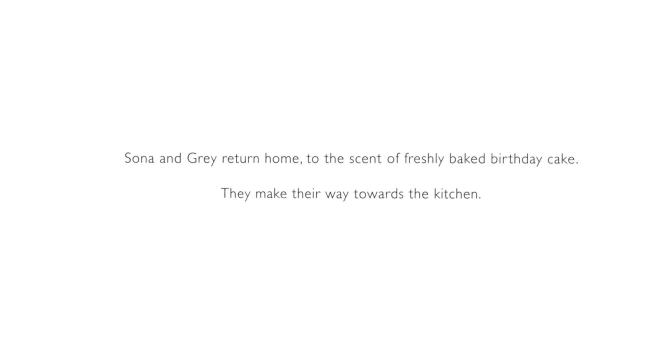

Sona and Grey return home, to the scent of freshly baked birthday cake.

They make their way towards the kitchen.

Sona sits down with her mum and dad, to eat cake and open her gift.

She wonders if there will be a silver balloon inside the box.

Her mind is full of travels with Grey.

Sona wonders when her next adventure will be.

Her next adventure is just a balloon away.

This book is dedicated to my parents, who fostered my love of travel.

Words by Rosa Park

Illustrations by Charles Finlay, based on **original drawings** by Clara Park

Art Direction and **Book Design** by Rich Stapleton

ISBN 978-1-9998218-3-8
©2018 Rosa Park

First published in 2018 by FRANCIS
1 Park Street, Bath, BA1 2TA, UK

Printed in the United Kingdom by Taylor Brothers.

rosa-park.com